THIS IS HAMMY, THE PET HAMSTER OF A BOY CALLED TIMMY THOMPSON. AND HAMMY HAS A DREAM...

I'M BORED GOING ROUND ON THIS WHEEL ALL DAY. I WISH I COULD DO SOMETHING ELSE. I WISH I COULD BE A SUPERHERO!

I REMEMBER HOW MY FATHER WAS BITTEN BY A RADIOACTIVE HAMSTER, GIVING HIM THE POWERS OF A HAMSTER. BUT HE WAS ALREADY A HAMSTER, SO THAT WAS NOT MUCH HELP.

OUCH!

IT'S NO GOOD. I'M NOT EVEN STRONG ENOUGH TO GET OUT OF THIS CAGE!

DON'T GIVE UP, HAMMY! WHO KNOWS WHAT WILL HAPPEN?

THE END... (NEARLY)

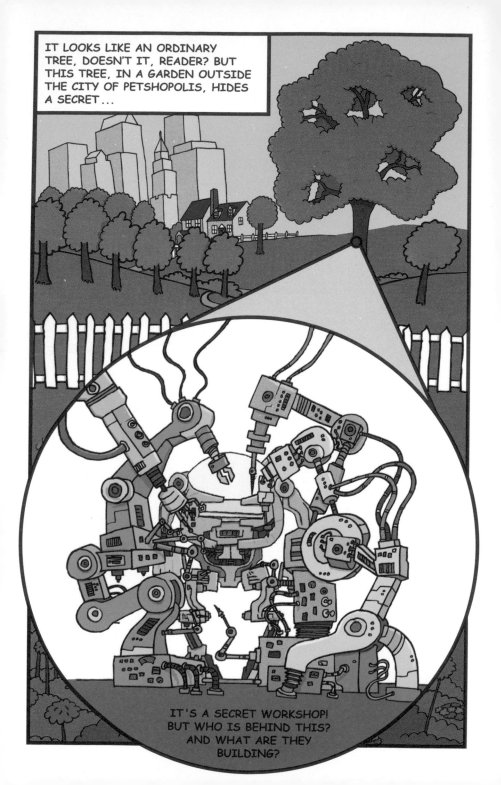

SUDDENLY, HE STARTS TO COUGH.

YUCK! BUT WHAT IS THIS CRIMINAL KITTY-KAT PLANNING?

*LOOK OUT FOR THESE CATS AGAIN IN THE FURRY FREEDOM FIGHTERS: ALL HAIL THE JELLYFIEND.

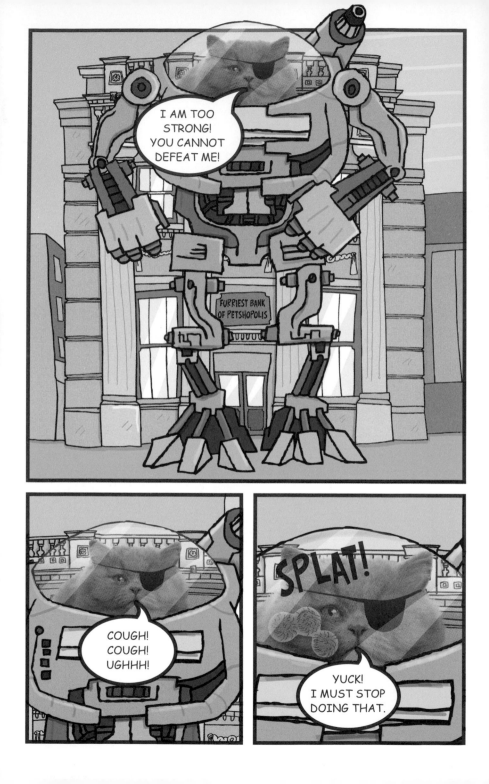

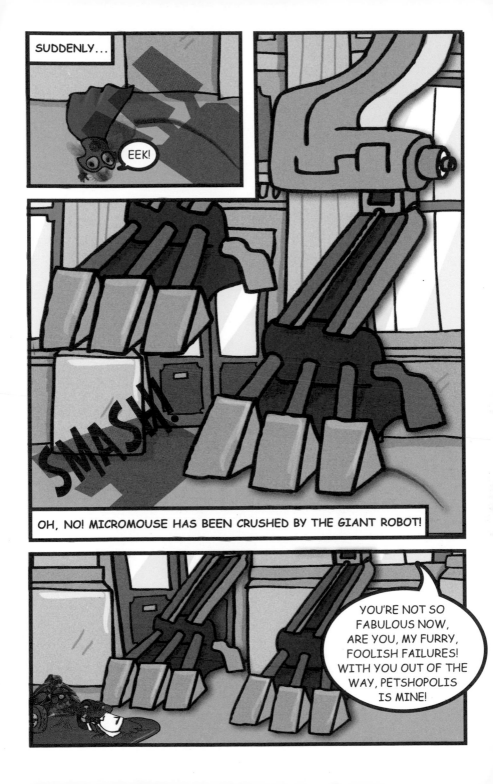

BUT WAIT!

GROAN! WHAT HAS HAPPENED TO ME!

BLINK! BLINK!

I'M...I'M, STILL ALIVE!

YES, READER, MICROMOUSE IS STILL ALIVE! THERE WAS A SMALL HOLE IN THE BOTTOM OF THE ROBOT'S FOOT, AND OUR TINY HERO CRAWLED THROUGH IT AND INTO THE ROBOT.

HOLE IN THE BOTTOM OF THE ROBOT'S FOOT.

INSIDE THE ROBOT:

OH, I'M SO TINY, WHAT CAN I DO? THIS IS SUCH A BIG ROBOT, AND IT IS CONTROLLED BY A CAT!

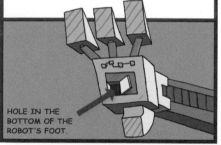

BE BRAVE, MICROMOUSE! NEVER GIVE UP! NO MATTER HOW SMALL YOU ARE, YOU CAN ALWAYS MAKE A DIFFERENCE!

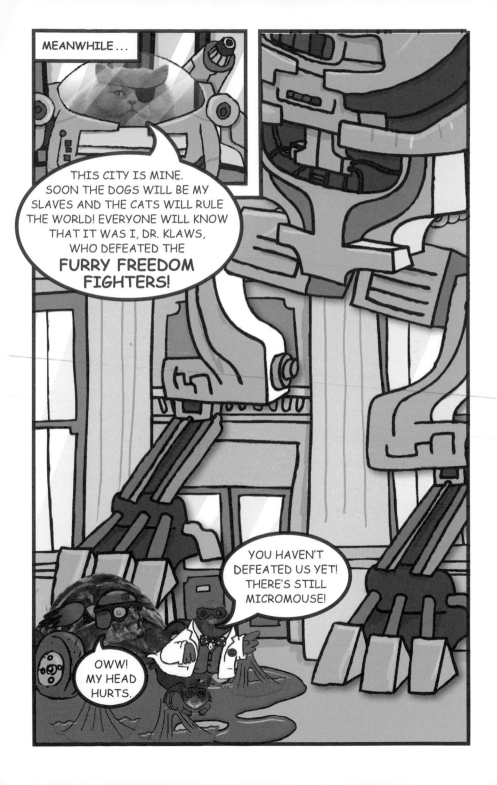

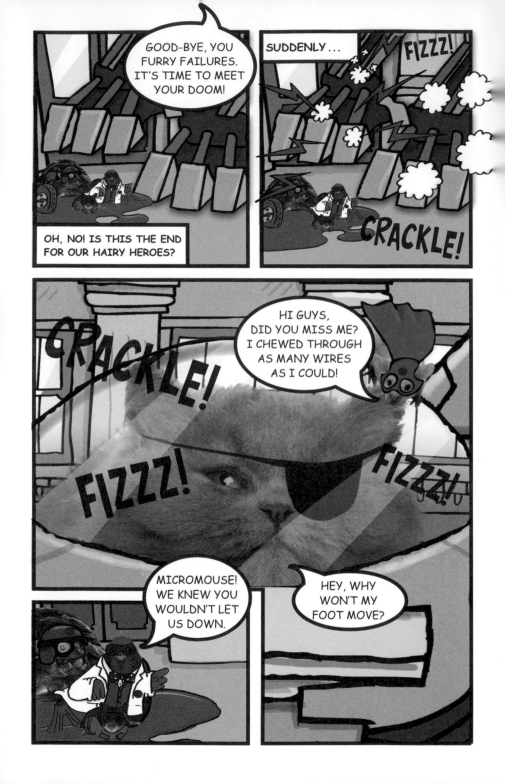

WHO'S THE FASTEST? WHO'S THE STRONGEST?

WHO'S THE MOST EVIL?

FIND OUT MORE ABOUT
THE FURRY FREEDOM FIGHTERS
AND THEIR FEARSOME FOES!

BIRDBRAIN

BIRDBRAIN COMES FROM THE MYSTERIOUS KINGDOM OF THE BIRDS. NOT JUST A FAMOUS INVENTOR, HE IS ALSO THE BRAINS BEHIND THE FURRY FREEDOM FIGHTERS.

REAL NAME: TOO HARD TO PRONOUNCE!

BRAINS: ★★★★★

STRENGTH: ★

SPEED: ★★

WEAPONS: ★★★

SURPRISE: ★★★

WEAKNESS: HE MAY BE BRAINY, BUT HE'S JUST A BIRD, SO HE CAN BE OVERPOWERED BY STRONG ENEMIES.

MICROMOUSE

WHILE ESCAPING FROM A SECRET LABORATORY, MICROMOUSE WAS HIT BY A SHRINKING RAY, GIVING HIM THE ABILITY TO TURN SUPER-SMALL AND GO SUPER-FAST!

REAL NAME: UNKNOWN

BRAINS: ★★

STRENGTH: ★

SPEED: ★★★★★

WEAPONS: ★

SURPRISE: ★★★★★

WEAKNESS: CHEESE — HE CAN'T RESIST IT! AND WHEN HE IS MICRO-SIZE, HE ALWAYS RUNS THE RISK OF BEING STEPPED ON.

TURBO TORTOISE

SECRET GOVERNMENT AGENT, TERRY TORTOISE,
WAS TURNED INTO A WALKING TIME BOMB BY
THE EVIL SQUIRREL, DR. NUTTY!

REAL NAME: TERRY TORTOISE

BRAINS: ★★★

STRENGTH: ★★★★★

SPEED: ★★★★

WEAPONS: ★★★★★

SURPRISE: ★★★

WEAKNESS: BEING TIPPIED OVER! LIKE ALL
TORTOISES, IF YOU TIP HIM OVER,
HE HAS PROBLEMS GETTING UP AGAIN!

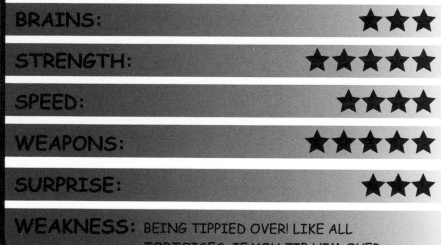

SUPERHAMMY

SUPERHAMMY IS THE SUPER-POWERED HAMSTER.
HE CAN FLY THROUGH THE AIR, HE CAN TEAR UP WHOLE
TREES — WHAT MORE COULD YOU WANT FROM A HAMSTER?

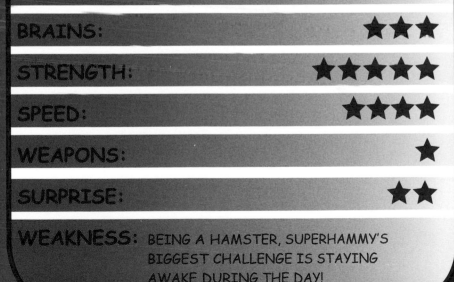

REAL NAME: HAMMY THE HAMSTER

BRAINS: ★★★

STRENGTH: ★★★★★

SPEED: ★★★★

WEAPONS: ★

SURPRISE: ★★

WEAKNESS: BEING A HAMSTER, SUPERHAMMY'S
BIGGEST CHALLENGE IS STAYING
AWAKE DURING THE DAY!

DR. KLAWS

THIS PEDIGREE CAT IS A FIENDISH INVENTOR.
HE TRIED TO DEFEAT THE FURRY FREEDOM
FIGHTERS BY BUILDING A ROBOT.

REAL NAME: PRINCE TIDDLES DE CREAMPUFF III

BRAINS: ★★★★★

STRENGTH: ★

SPEED: ★★

WEAPONS: ★★★★★

SURPRISE: ★★★

WEAKNESS: HAIR BALLS — LIKE ALL CATS, HE JUST
CAN'T STOP COUGHING THEM UP.

THE RED FANG

THIS MAD MANIAC TURNED THE HUNGRY
MEERKATS INTO AN ARMY AND THEN MARCHED
THEM INTO PETSHOPOLIS!

REAL NAME: ERICH VON STOATWEASEL

BRAINS: ★★★★

STRENGTH: ★

SPEED: ★★

WEAPONS: ★★★★★

SURPRISE: ★★★★

WEAKNESS: HIS OWN BIG HEAD! HE THINKS
THAT HE CAN NEVER BE DEFEATED,
BUT THAT'S WHERE HE IS WRONG!

THE MEERKAT ARMY

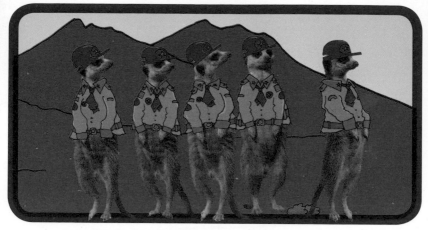

THE MEERKATS WERE PERSUADED TO ATTACK PETSHOPOLIS BY THE RED FANG, BUT ALL THEY WANTED WAS SOMETHING TO EAT.

REAL NAME: TOO MANY TO MENTION

BRAINS: ★

STRENGTH: ★★

SPEED: ★★

WEAPONS: ★

SURPRISE: ★★

WEAKNESS: THEY ARE NOT THE SMARTEST OF ANIMALS!